To Matthew Jon
Love from Grandpa
Grandma and Grandpa
December 2011

The Legend of
HOBBOMOCK
The Sleeping Giant

Story by JASON J. MARCHI

Illustrated by JESSE J. BONELLI

Fahrenheit Books

NEW HAVEN, CONNECTICUT

Published by Fahrenheit Books™
An imprint of OmicronWorld Entertainment LLC.
32 Alfred Street, Suite B
New Haven, CT 06512-3927
www.OmicronWorld.com
OmicronWorldEnt@yahoo.com

Cover and Interior Design by Thomas Goddard

Text: Caslon
CPSIA Compliance Information: Batch 0911
For further information contact RJ Communications. Phone: 800.621.2556.
MANUFACTURED IN THE UNITED STATES OF AMERICA

ISBN: 978-0-9830945-1-7

FIRST PRINTING, October 2011
10 9 8 7 6 5 4 3 2 1

SOURCES:
The Algonquin Confederacy of the Quinnipiac Tribal Council – Iron Thunderhorse, www.acqtc.org
The Sleeping Giant Park Association, www.sgpa.org
Yale Peabody Museum of Natural History, peabody.yale.edu
Mashantucket Pequot Museum and Research Center, www.pequotmuseum.org
The National Geographic Society, www.nationalgeographic.com

ACKNOWLEDGEMENTS:
Additional thanks are due to those who gave advice, information, and encouragement during the writing of
this book: Fawn Murphy, Karen Jensen, Sascha Gardiner, Don Rankin, Paula Feder, and Cynthia Dubea.

This is the first book in the Local Legends™ series of educational children's books.
Visit www.omicronworld.com to order a parent/teacher guide to utilize this book.

DEDICATION

For
Jeanne Roche Whalen
who first told me of the legend of
the Sleeping Giant in the summer of 1976.

And for
Dale Carson
who, in 2006, set me on the final path to find my
own story amidst the differing versions of the legend.
-JJM

To my mentors William Allik and Nicholas Evans-Cato,
my grandfather John McCaffery,
and for Liz Mooney.
-JJB

IN days long ago many Native American people believed that giants made from stone once roamed the earth.

One such stone giant was called Hobbomock.

Hobbomock lived on the Long Water Land with a Native American people who called themselves the Quinnipiac.

Like all giants, Hobbomock ate a lot of food, spoke loud as thunder, and shook the earth when he walked.

A young Quinnipiac boy called Blackbird, first heard stories about Hobbomock from his elders.

One such elder was Rakarota, a master storyteller.

"Hobbomock was our cultural hero," said Rakarota to Blackbird and others in his clan. All were seated before a warming fire in the clan's longhouse.

"Hobbomock taught the Quinnipiac people to hunt and fish," continued the storyteller. "He taught them to care for the land and the water. He taught them that all things are sacred."

Blackbird listened carefully while Rakarota spoke.

"When Hobbomock lived among our ancestors the winged people (the birds) and the four-legged people (the animals) and the two-legged people (the humans) all spoke the same language.

"Harmony and peace were everywhere.

"One day Hobbomock sailed away in his stone canoe to teach other peoples who lived far away how to hunt and fish and care for their land."

"What happened after Hobbomock went away?" Blackbird interrupted.

Rakarota smiled at Blackbird.

"While Hobbomock was away," Rakarota continued, "the land of our ancestors changed. After the sun and moon rose and fell many, many times the birds, the animals, and the humans no longer spoke the same language. They could not understand each other so fear and distrust came to the land of the Quinnipiac. When Hobbomock finally returned he grew angry at our ancestors."

"What did he do then?" Blackbird asked.

"To show his anger Hobbomock stamped his foot and the earth shook," Rakarota said. "He stamped his foot into the long river of pines and caused the river to change direction. Today the river still makes a sharp turn where Hobbomock stamped his foot."

"What did Hobbomock do next?" Blackbird asked.

Blackbird's mother hushed the boy.

"You are ever the inquisitive one," Rakarota said, and he now spoke directly to Blackbird.

"Hobbomock was so angry with our ancestors he went away again. But legend foretells that Hobbomock said he would come back and punish our people for not respecting the birds in the sky and the animals in the forest," the storyteller said.

After Rakarota finished his story Blackbird went to sleep and dreamed of the stone giant Hobbomock. He hoped he would never see Hobbomock return to punish his people.

Many seasons passed—winters, springs, summers, and autumns— and when Blackbird was a few years older he was allowed to journey into the woods on his own.

Blackbird nearly forgot about the stone giant Hobbomock, for Rakarota told many more exciting legends.

ONE morning Blackbird woke to fill his lungs with the cool morning air and feel the first warm rays of the sun on his face.

He put on his leather breechcloths and leggings, slipped on a pair of buckskin moccasins, and grabbed the bow and arrows his grandfather had made for him.

After a breakfast of corn, beans, and squash—and fresh oysters his mother had gathered earlier that morning from the edge of the Long Water—Blackbird said goodbye to his mother and father for the day and walked into the deep forest alone.

Before long, Blackbird spotted a squirrel.

He followed the squirrel until a deer appeared in the forest.

He followed the deer through the forest until a hawk appeared in the sky.

Blackbird followed the hawk along a stream, over a hill, into a valley, and up another hill until he reached the edge of the long river of pines.

The hawk disappeared into the tree tops on the other side of the river.

While Blackbird watched the slow river, he felt a mystical presence. He felt like he was one with the Spirit World.

Suddenly his peaceful feeling was shattered when the earth shook for a moment, followed by silence.

The land shook again after the sound of a distant boom.

The booming sound continued and drew closer. The earth shook more violently after each boom.

Blackbird was about to run when the booming sounds stopped.

The earth was still again.

Blackbird stood very still for he thought he saw something move among the trees at the edge of the river.

The thing that moved did not look like a squirrel, or a deer, or even a bird. In fact, Blackbird could not tell what it was among the trees until he heard a loud cracking sound overhead—the sound of large tree branches snapping—and he looked up.

There, towering overhead, high above the trees, was a giant man made of stone!

"Hobbomock?!" Blackbird blurted out loud.

The stone giant heard the human voice, and turned his dark and angular face to look down at Blackbird.

Blackbird began to tremble.

The giant reached for the boy with a stony fist the size of a boulder and Blackbird ran. He ran with like a frightened deer, away from the river and into the forest.

Hobbomock followed, his giant stone feet smashing trees like they were twigs.

For every twenty running strides Blackbird took, Hobbomock drew closer with a single, giant step.

Blackbird stopped, drew an arrow from its quiver, and fumbled to place it on the bow string.

Hobbomock stopped and looked down at Blackbird who had dropped the arrow and was now frozen still, like a startled rabbit.

"Why have you come to the edge of this river?" thundered Hobbomock's voice.

Blackbird hesitated a moment then puffed out his chest to make his tiny body look bigger.

"I have come to explore and to hunt," Blackbird said.

"You cannot hunt along this river!" Hobbomock thundered. "This is my river and your people no longer respect it. You no longer speak the same language as the birds and the animals."

"I do respect the river," Blackbird said. "I respect the squirrel I followed, and the deer in the forest, and the hawk that flew here to the river."

"I will hear no more!" the giant's voice boomed, and he stomped his foot. The ground shook and Blackbird fell backward. He jumped back to his feet, unharmed, and ran.

Hobbomock stomped the ground again and again, crushing tree after tree, looking for Blackbird. But the boy was gone.

When Blackbird arrived back at his clan he ran straight to his mother and father.

"Where have you been?" his mother asked. "We heard great thunder in the distance. We were concerned about you, Blackbird."

"It's not thunder you heard. I went to the river and I saw him. I saw the stone giant, Hobbomock. He was angry and stomped his feet and he told me I could not hunt by the river because our people no longer respect the land and the animals. Where is Rakarota? I must tell him that Hobbomock has returned to punish us."

Hearing the commotion, Rakarota had come to Blackbird's longhouse and he was already standing in the doorway.

"Rakarota, Rakarota," Blackbird panted, "that was not thunder you heard. The stone giant Hobbomock has returned, just as you said he would."

"Hobbomock tried to hurt you?" Rakarota asked.

"He tried to grab me but I ran. And he stomped the trees with his giant stone feet and tried to crush me."

"Did he see which way you ran?"

"I don't think so," Blackbird said. "I ran like my father taught me. I ran like the rabbit, in a circle, and then I went off in the opposite direction and came home."

"That will give us some time," Blackbird's father said, "but we must stop Hobbomock before he finds us."

"There is only one thing we can do to stop Hobbomock," Rakarota said. "We must summon the good spirit Keitan and ask for his help."

Blackbird's father gathered the elders while Rakarota gathered his charms: a bear's claw, a fox's tooth, and a bird's foot.

The elders—both women and men—sat in a circle around the charms and began to chant. Blackbird sat between his father and his grandfather. Together, they chanted the ancient words to summon the good spirit Keitan.

Keitan could not be seen, but he could be heard in the whispers of the nearby fire. The elders asked Keitan to cast a spell to stop Hobbomock from hurting their people. While they chanted they heard the thunder and felt the ground shake as Hobbomock drew closer, looking for Blackbird.

Keitan knew that giants need a lot of food, and he knew that Hobbomock's favorite food was oysters. So he cast a sleeping spell on the oysters along the edge of the Long Water.

The booming footsteps of the giant came closer, closer…and then they stopped.

The elders went silent, ending the chant.

They listened.

Blackbird left the longhouse and climbed to the top of a tall oak tree. He whispered down to the others who had followed him and now stood at the base of the tree.

"I see him," Blackbird said. "I see Hobbomock at the edge of the Long Water. He's scooping up the oysters and eating."

This pleased Rakarota. What Keitan had said from the whispers of the fire was true. Hobbomock had grown very hungry and he needed to stop for food—for oysters—before continuing his search for Blackbird.

Once Hobbomock was full of oysters, he yawned and blew out a giant breath. His breath made the treetops swayed back and forth.

He took three giant steps, shook the ground, stopped, and yawned. The sound of a thunderous growl came from his mouth.

The giant took two more steps, stopped, and yawned again.

And then he took one small step, stopped, and lifted his stone hands to his stone face.

Hobbomock stood very still, not moving.

He began to teeter, and then he fell to his knees in a thunderous bang.

Hobbomock knelt for a long count, still holding his hands to his face. His arms then dropped to his sides and he rolled sideways and fell onto his back in one final explosion of shaking earth.

The earth shook so violently Blackbird fell from the tree. He broke his fall by grabbing onto branches and landed on the soft forest floor, unharmed.

Hobbomock, the stone giant, lay on his back, fast asleep under the power of Keitan's sleeping spell.

"Hobbomock cannot punish us now," Blackbird said.

"He will sleep for a long, long time," Rakarota said, and he smiled at Blackbird.

The years passed while Hobbomock slept.

The forest that Blackbird once played in and hunted in grew over Hobbomock while he slept.

When Blackbird grew older he became a father and a grandfather himself. When Rakarota died Blackbird took his place as a master storyteller among the Quinnipiac people.

Blackbird told his clan of the old legend of the stone giant Hobbomock as Rakarota had told it. And he told them of the new legend— of the time when Hobbomock returned to punish Blackbird and his people, and how the good spirit Keitan cast a sleeping spell to put Hobbomock to sleep for a long, long time.

Today, Hobbomock still sleeps. His sleeping body lies beneath the set of hills that form the Sleeping Giant landform in what is now Hamden, Connecticut.

But legend has it that one day Keitan's sleeping spell will wear off... and Hobbomock will wake up... and the hills that form his head, his body, and his legs will be gone.

And legend also has it that when Hobbomock wakes up... he will be very, very hungry.

Afterword

IN the Mount Carmel section of Hamden, Connecticut there is a landscape feature that forms the shape of a giant man sleeping on his back. One short hill forms the head, one medium hill forms the body, and one long hill forms the legs. The Sleeping Giant stretches over two miles in length from head to toe.

This book tells a story of how those hills came to be formed. The story is based upon three differing versions of the legend of the Sleeping Giant as passed down from both the Native American people who called themselves the Quinnipiac and the early European settlers known as the Puritans who put their own spin on the story.

The author has taken a few creative liberties in the retelling of this legend, but he has also attempted to stay as true as possible to the oral traditions of the Quinnipiac people—and to the details of how they lived—as passed down from one generation to the next over the past 350 years and as recorded by the European settlers.